A Flower in the Snow

Tracey Corderoy   Sophie Allsopp

EGMONT

In an icy kingdom, far away, lived a little girl called Luna.

Her happy smile sparkled
like the snow.

Luna loved to dance through
the snowflakes, or catch them
on her tongue...

A C

Snow

For Anna, who has always loved Bear
All my love
T.C. xx

For the bears in my family
S.A.

EGMONT

We bring stories to life

Our story began over a century ago, when seventeen-year-old
Egmont Harald Petersen found a coin in the street.

He was on his way to buy a flyswatter, a small hand-operated
printing machine that he then set up in his tiny apartment.

The coin brought him such good luck that today Egmont has
offices in over 30 countries around the world. And that lucky
coin is still kept at the company's head offices in Denmark.

First published in Great Britain 2012
by Egmont UK Limited 239 Kensington High Street, London W8 6SA

www.egmont.co.uk

Text copyright © 2012 Tracey Corderoy
Illustrations copyright © 2012 Sophie Allsopp

The moral rights of the author and illustrator have been asserted

ISBN 978 1 4052 4944 7 (Hardback)
ISBN 978 1 4052 4945 4 (Paperback)
ISBN 978 1 7803 1249 1 (Ebook)

1 3 5 7 9 10 8 6 4 2

A CIP catalogue record for this title is available from the British Library

Printed and bound in Singapore

46321/1/2

... or leave little tiptoe patterns everywhere!

But there was one thing Luna loved more than all of these. He was big and soft and cuddly and was Luna's best friend...

Bear.

Luna and Bear belonged together, like bread and strawberry jam!

And everything they did, they did together.

Skating on the frozen lake ...

...rolling giant snowballs,

or even
catching
a cold!

Luna lived in an igloo and Bear lived in a snow cave in her little garden where, one bright day, something most unusual popped up. It was a flower - a dancing yellow flower!

How pretty it is, thought Bear.

Then, carefully, he picked it for someone special.

"Just look at its face!" smiled Luna.
"My little sunshine flower!
I've never seen anything so
beautiful – I'll treasure it
forever!"

But, all too soon, her flower
wilted, and as the last petal
fell, so Luna's sparkly smile
disappeared.

And nothing…

would bring it back.

Finally Bear knew what he had to do to bring back Luna's smile. So away he sailed to find another sunshine flower.

The next day Luna searched
everywhere for Bear. Then,
at last, she found a note.

Gone to find a
sunshine flower.
Bear x x

From then on, every night, Luna would gaze at the moon.
"Please come home tomorrow, Bear," she'd whisper.

And, every morning, she'd rush to his
cave and peep through the little window.

"Bear!" she'd call ...

... but he was never there.

Far, far away, Bear searched for his special gift for Luna.

Along dusty, windswept tracks...

on through deep, dark jungles...

down soft, grassy
hillsides …

and across hot, sandy deserts.
But, though he hunted high and low …

...he couldn't find a sunshine flower.

Then, one crisp and twinkly night,
a snowflake kissed his nose.

How good it felt - so cold and light!
It was time to go home to Luna.

So Bear set sail once again and tall
waves tossed his boat.

Through days and nights
he held on tight ...

...until, at last, he landed
on the icy shores of home.

Bear was sad that he had no gift for Luna,
but seeing her again was all that mattered.

But Luna wasn't dancing through
the snowflakes, or making tiptoe
patterns in the snow like she used to.

And then he saw her!

"Bear!" cried Luna. "You've come home!"

"But I haven't brought your gift," Bear answered sadly.
"Oh, Bear," smiled Luna. "You are my gift!
As long as you are here with me, I'm happy."

"Bear, come with me,"
she said, taking his
big, soft paw. "There's
something very
special I have
to show you!"

"When the last petal fell from the sunshine
flower, some little seeds were left.
So I planted one," smiled Luna,
"and watered it every day!
And look what grew …

… *another* sunshine flower!"

Then, from her pocket, she took
Bear's note and carefully unwrapped it.

"I've been saving these seeds
to plant with you," she said.

So Luna and Bear planted the
seeds and cared for them each day.
And, before long…

. . . . a sunshine meadow

And hiding among the flowers were butterflies and bees,

...anced in the snow!

snails and spotty ladybirds and ...

...two very best of friends.